This Walker book

belongs to:

For my husband, James,
and for Mum and Dad – thank you

First published 2013 by Walker Books Ltd
87 Vauxhall Walk, London SE11 5HJ

This edition published 2014

2 4 6 8 10 9 7 5 3 1

This book has been typeset in Myriad Tilt

Printed in China

British Library Cataloguing in Publication Data:
a catalogue record for this book is available from the British Library

ISBN 978-1-4063-5255-9

www.walker.co.uk

THE
BLACK RABBIT

Philippa Leathers

WALKER BOOKS

AND SUBSIDIARIES

LONDON · BOSTON · SYDNEY · AUCKLAND

RABBIT WOKE UP ONE MORNING and stepped out of his burrow into the bright sunlight. It was a beautiful day.

But something was wrong.
He was not alone.

Rabbit was scared.

"Go away, Black Rabbit!" he cried.

But the Black Rabbit did not move.

Rabbit ran.

But the Black Rabbit was right behind him.

Rabbit ran even faster.

The Black Rabbit won't find me here! thought Rabbit,
and he hid behind a tree.

But when Rabbit stepped out from behind the tree . . .

there was the Black Rabbit right in front of him!

Maybe he is not a good swimmer like me, thought Rabbit, and he jumped into the river and swam to the other side.

But as he pulled himself up onto the bank . . .

the Black Rabbit climbed out of the water too!

"What do you want?"
cried Rabbit, trembling.
"Why are you following me?"

But the Black Rabbit did not reply.

Rabbit began to run again, faster than he had ever run before – straight into the deep, dark wood.

WELCOME to the deep, DARK WOOD

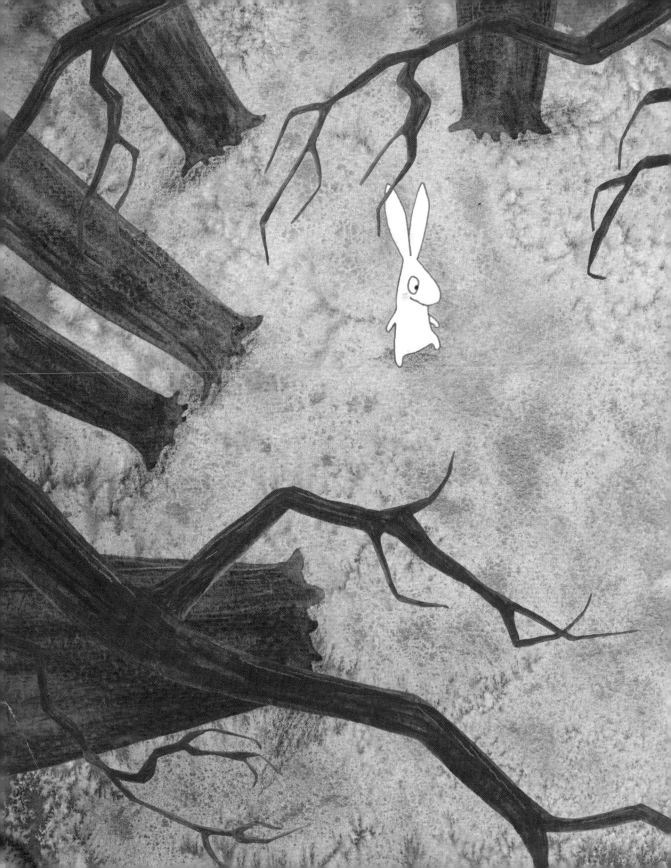

The forest was dark and quiet.
The Black Rabbit was nowhere to be seen.

With a sigh of relief,
Rabbit sat down and
nibbled a carrot . . .

until he noticed two eyes shining brightly in the dark.

OH, NO, thought Rabbit. *The Black Rabbit has found me.*

But it was NOT the Black Rabbit.

Rabbit ran as fast as he could out of the deep, dark forest,
with Wolf close behind him.

Then he tripped!

Rabbit scrambled to his feet, but it was too late.

He shut his eyes tight and waited for Wolf to attack...

But nothing happened.

Because there, standing in the sunlight behind Rabbit, was the Black Rabbit.

Rabbit smiled, and somehow he knew that the
Black Rabbit was smiling back.
Hand in hand, they bounced off across the field.

PHILIPPA LEATHERS studied graphic design, illustration and animation, and now works as a freelance animator and illustrator. **The Black Rabbit** is her first picture book. She lives in Kent with her husband and two daughters, a grey tabby cat named Emmi, and two rabbits called Benji and Kiki, who inspired her to write this book – since where one goes, the other follows close behind.

Available from all good booksellers

www.walker.co.uk